THE SEER

A PREQUEL TO THE STONE OF KNOWING

ALLAN N. PACKER

LUMINANT PUBLICATIONS

*'The Seer' is dedicated to Ali, so generous with her words, and already such
an encouragement.*

Castel
Castel Citadel
Deadman's Pass
Steffan's Citadel
Arven
Maranelle
Duchy
of
Erestor
N
W
E
S
Arvenon
& surrounding Kingdoms

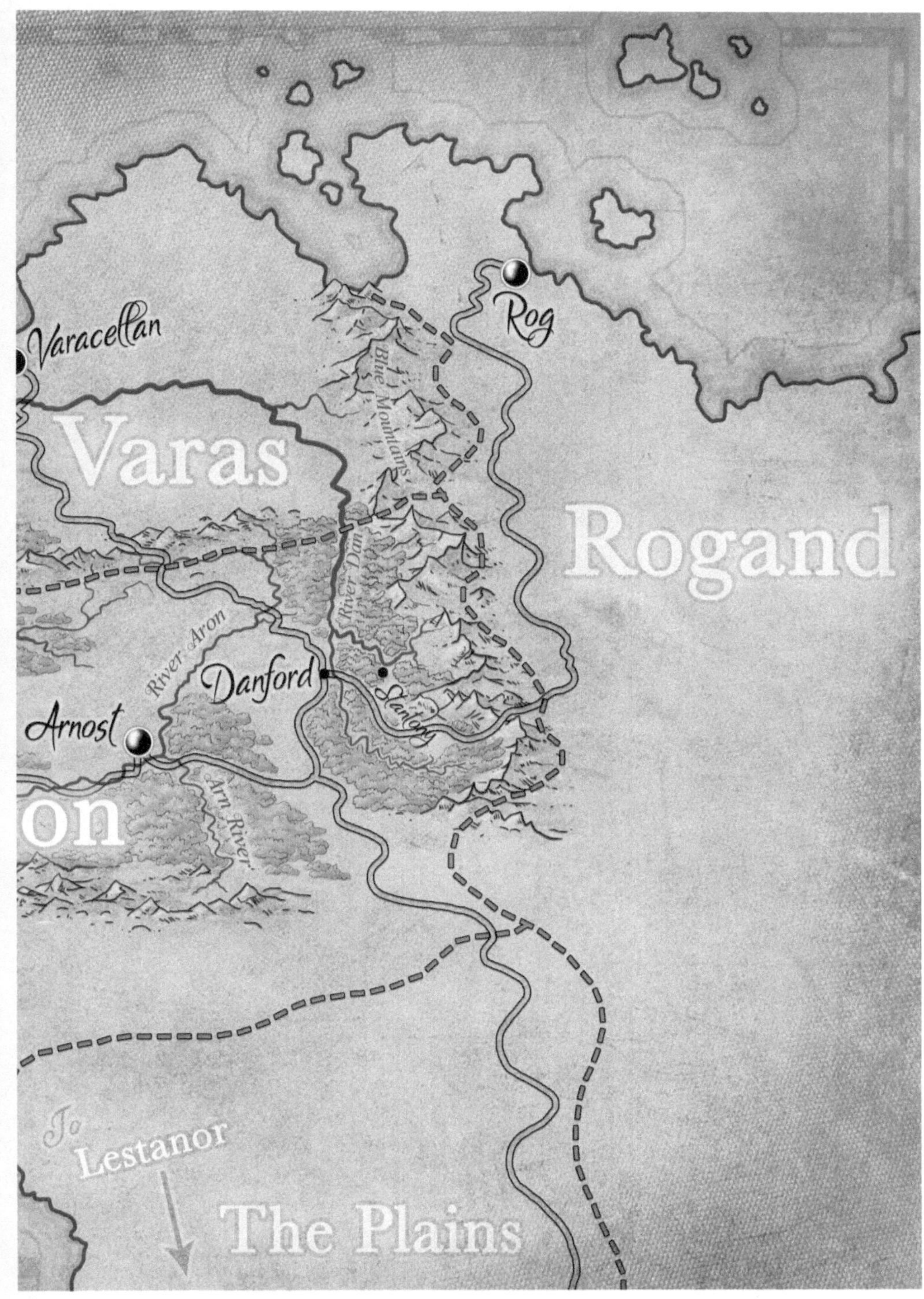

Varacellan
Rog
Varas
Rogand
River Aron
River Dan
Blue Mountains
Danford
Llanon
Arnost
Arn River
on
To Lestanor
The Plains

1

Kalvor bent low to the ground, studying the signs. To his practiced eye they were easy to read. Not just one person, but several had passed this way. Recently. The village must be nearby. His quarry was surely within reach at last.

For months he had searched for the woman. At first his efforts had been entirely in vain. Later he had little more to go on than hints and vague whispers. Kalvor had not been dismayed. There was a reason Lord Drettroth chose him for this kind of assignment.

The hunt had led him south beyond the borders of Rogand, deep into the northern forests of Lestanor. The woman he sought avoided towns and cities, choosing instead to live in lightly populated areas. But the entire region was filled with the rumor of her. Either she knew nothing about hiding herself effectively, or she didn't bother to try. She was foolish indeed if she didn't try.

Remaining hidden would have required her to stop using her special gift. Apparently that was a limitation she was unwilling to accept.

It still wasn't easy to find her. No one would tell him exactly where she was. The common people revered her and protected her, even at personal risk to themselves. A string of violent encounters had testified to that. Her talents were in demand, though, and her visitors left trails for those able to read them.

He wondered if she knew he was coming for her. Perhaps she would flee. He licked his lips involuntarily at the prospect—hunting was so much more satisfying when the rabbit decided to run. It wouldn't save her. He was no ordinary hunter—he was the best. And he never gave up.

THE SUN HAD BARELY RISEN when Kalvor finally reached the location he had been seeking. The village stood beside a small river, consisting of little more than a few rude huts. Between the huts and the river lay a cultivated patch protected from the river by a simple levee. He observed the village from a distance for the entire morning, staying out of sight. None of the villagers appeared to be armed—they were woefully unprepared for the arrival of someone like him.

He saw no sign of the woman. If she was in the village, though, it wasn't difficult to guess where she might be. One of the huts was attracting much more than its share of attention. People had come and gone constantly as he watched.

He waited until the sun had passed its zenith, then he simply walked into the village. He didn't doubt for a moment his ability to deal with whatever he might find there.

He went straight to the hut he had been watching. Without introduction or ceremony, he stooped down and stepped through the low entrance. A small group—an old man, a couple of children, and a woman—sat around a rough wooden table. He knew immediately she was the one Lord Drettroth wanted. There was an air about her, something indefinable that set her apart.

A frown creased the brow of the old man when Kalvor appeared. The children simply gazed up curiously at the newcomer. As for the woman, she didn't seem surprised by his arrival. Her face revealed no concern at all. She simply looked at him, studying him calmly without speaking.

He stared back at her. The woman was probably in her early thirties. She was almost certainly not Rogandan—she lacked the dark hair that characterized his race. She wasn't beautiful, although her brown curls fell attractively enough about her face, and there was something pleasing about the fullness of her lips. He registered all of this impassively—he had no interest in her as a person.

"Please join us," she said calmly, speaking to him in Rogandan, his mother tongue. She waved to an empty seat opposite her at the table. "We're about to share a simple meal together."

His lips curled back in a smile. Why not? His victims didn't usually feed him before he dragged them away, but he was hungry, and more than willing to make an exception.

She said a few words to the old man in the language of Lestanor. He nodded once, and left the table to fetch fresh milk, a loaf of bread, and a cluster of dates. Depositing them in the center of the table, he sat down once again, eyeing the newcomer suspiciously.

They ate together in silence. The old man looked troubled. The children stole curious glances in Kalvor's direction from time to time. The woman's eyes never left him.

When the food had almost been consumed, she broke the silence. "He never hated you," she said, addressing him once again in Rogandan.

Kalvor frowned in puzzlement. He had no idea what she was talking about.

"Your brother," she said. "He never hated you."

He scowled at her. She was a seer, of course—it was the one thing everyone agreed on. But he hadn't hunted her down so she could poke around in the dung heap of his past. Perhaps she was trying to put him on the defensive, to weaken him. If so, she was wasting her time.

"I didn't come here to talk about my brother," he told her curtly.

"No," she said quietly. "I know why you're here."

"Then it won't surprise you to know that I'm leaving, now, and you're coming with me." His hand moved to the hilt of his sword. "Do I need to explain why it will be better for your friends here if you don't argue?"

"No." She shook her head. "I fully understand what you're capable of."

"Good. Then you'll be sensible and come quietly."

The old man made to get out of his chair. He clearly had not understood the words they had spoken, but he seemed to grasp the general idea well enough. The woman addressed him rapidly in his own tongue. Kalvor knew a little of the language of Lestanor, but she spoke too quickly for him to catch it all. He thought she was telling him she couldn't stay there anyway.

The old man protested, but she shook her head firmly. Rising from the table, she embraced him briefly, then said goodbye to the children after kissing them both on the head.

"I'm ready," she announced. "Can I get a few things?"

"Make it quick. I'll come with you—I'm not letting you out of my sight."

He followed her around closely as she gathered some food and a few items of clothing and put them into a sack.

The moment she was ready he led her away from the village, avoiding established paths.

Once they had made a start, he found himself impatient to be away from there. They moved quickly, traveling until the afternoon was spent. Then he found a sheltered spot beside a stream and instructed her to sit. He didn't bother with a fire—he had nothing to cook, and they weren't lacking in warmth given the balmy weather.

The woman produced a loaf of bread from the bundle in her sack and broke it into two, handing him a piece. "My name is Sheylha," she said.

He took the bread with a grunt. He didn't offer his own name.

She watched him quietly again. Then she said, "Some men might come after me. If they do, please let me handle it. I can negotiate with them."

"I don't negotiate. If anyone comes, I'll deal with them my way."

Her brow furrowed. "Disagreeing with someone doesn't mean you need to kill them."

He snorted. "Disagreements should never be left to fester. I learned that the hard way."

She fell silent.

"Who are these men?" he asked. "What do they want with you?" It didn't hurt to be prepared.

She paused for a moment. "Their leader wants me, for my...gift."

He didn't respond.

"Your Lord Drettroth isn't the only one who wants to control me," she added.

So she knew who had sent him. The ambitious Rogandan lord must have had dealings with her in the past. Curiosity flickered briefly in his mind, but he stomped it down quickly. What difference did it make?

When night fell she lay down and was soon asleep. Kalvor sat silent in the darkness, brooding.

HE TRUDGED WEARILY BACK to the campsite. The woman sat there quietly, peering curiously at him in the early dawn light. She frowned. "Are you hurt?"

Stepping over to the stream he splashed the blood off his clothes. Then he found a patch of grass and cleaned his sword. He didn't bother to answer.

"So they did come," she said simply. "Three of them."

Somehow she knew. She was a seer. "There will be more," he told her.

"Yes, there will," she said.

The day had only just begun, and already he felt tired. "Time we were going."

Sheylha nodded. She stood and followed him away from the stream.

THEY HAD CHANGED DIRECTION, heading directly away from the morning sun. "Where are we heading?" Sheylha asked curiously.

"West for a while. We're being tracked. I'm going to try to shake them off."

He left her late in the morning, heading back toward their pursuers. He expected to be gone for a while—a full day at least. It was possible she might try to run, but for some reason he didn't think so.

She'd been surprisingly cooperative. He couldn't account for it. It was almost as though she wanted to go with him. He pushed it from his mind, focusing instead on becoming the hunter rather than the hunted.

He located them early in the evening. There were twelve of them, and their numbers must have made them overconfident. They had stopped for the day and were making a lot of noise. They hadn't set sentries. He would teach them a valuable lesson that night.

Wild boar were foraging near their camp—Kalvor had seen their spoor. The creatures could be extremely dangerous when provoked, so he spent the next couple of hours locating a big one and provoking it. Then he let it chase him to the outskirts of the camp, swinging himself onto a low hanging tree branch at the last possible minute. The boar charged into the camp, causing instant chaos. When the confusion finally died down, two men lay seriously injured. The boar was responsible for that. Another three lay dead. He left the survivors to decide for themselves how that had happened.

Throughout the night Kalvor headed northeast, leaving a clear trail behind him. When he found a suitable opportunity, he doubled back. The trackers would eventually find that his trail had simply disappeared.

HE RETURNED to discover that Sheylha had indeed waited for him. They resumed their journey, heading west for three more days before swinging north. Crossing the border into Arvenon, they eventually made their way into the dense forests southeast of the town of Danford. Kalvor made camp with the intention of lying low for several days. He was confident that their new location in Arvenon would be extremely difficult to trace.

Having settled on a base, Kalvor addressed his attention to the problem of provisions. He set snares and gathered edible roots and wild berries.

Sheylha was both able and willing to assist with practicalities. He had never abducted anyone quite like her. She never descended into blubbering incapacity. She never even complained. She seemed to understand his moods better than he did himself, and knew when to speak and when to remain quiet.

A week stretched to two and then three, and still he did not resume their journey. He told himself he was simply being cautious. But it began to dawn on him that he might actually miss her company when the time came to hand her over to Drettroth. Alarmed at even the possibility of a sign of weakness, he determined to put her out of his mind entirely. Once it had become a conscious issue, though, the more he tried not to think about her the more impossible it became. Adopting the simplest solution of avoiding her, he took to spending large amounts of time away from their camp, testing a hunting bow and arrows he had recently fashioned.

One day he returned a little before noon to find Sheylha gone. A rapid inspection of the site revealed signs of a struggle. Furious with himself for his own foolishness, he immediately set out in pursuit. He quickly discovered he was tracking several men as well as the woman.

They were making no attempt to hide their tracks—they were in a race against time. His task would become much more difficult if he failed to reach them before darkness fell. Her captors would not stop when daylight ended, and he would be forced to wait until dawn to resume his tracking. By then they would be far away. He took comfort in the thought that however hard they drove her, the woman would still slow them down.

He could run through the forest like a deer, and follow a track from the faintest of signs. And he was angry now. He flew forward, passing through the trees like a breath of wind.

The sun was sinking low in the sky when he finally caught up with them. He counted six men, all part of the original group that had met the boar. They were more alert this time. Nevertheless, two of them went down with feathered arrows in their backs before they saw him. One remained with the woman, the other three attacked him together.

He threw down the bow and drew his sword. One came at him head on, while the other two closed in on each side. The location did not favor a group, though. They were attacking him among the trees, not in the open.

Kalvor lunged aggressively at the one in front, driving him back rapidly to keep him off balance. The defender soon stumbled onto a low shrub and lost his footing. Kalvor ran him through, then dived to the side as one of the remaining two tried to take advantage of his distraction. Both of them came at him at once. They clearly knew how to fight, and they were counting on overwhelming force to beat him down.

He had faced worse odds, though, and he was confident he was equal to the task. He was superbly fit, with rippling muscles and not an ounce of body fat, and his unusual height gave him superior reach. He settled into a familiar rhythm, allowing his arm to move his sword instinctively while he assessed their weaknesses.

"Kalvor, behind you!"

The warning shout shocked him into action. He feinted, then swung to one side, barely escaping a wild sword thrust from behind him. Sheylha's minder had joined the fight, and they came at him from all sides again. He ducked and weaved swiftly until he had placed a large tree at his back. Then he thrust forward, his sword flickering. He took the weakest of the three in the side, and the man crumpled with a cry. The others closed the gap and came at him together.

"Kalvor, behind you again!"

He registered—almost too late—that there were seven of them, not six. The seventh must have been scouting when he caught up with the main group.

Reversing his sword, he thrust it behind him. He got lucky, taking his new opponent by surprise. But while he was off guard, both of the others leaned forward and thrust at him together. One sword pierced his side and the other his right leg.

Searing pain overwhelmed his senses, and he almost blacked out. Grimacing, he somehow launched his sword at one of his two remaining attackers. The sword found its target, but Kalvor no longer had the strength to withdraw it. As the final attacker drew back his weapon for a killing thrust, Kalvor pulled his knife and threw it with the last of his failing energy. He pitched forward, his own blood spilling around him.

As blackness overtook him, his fading thought was one of wonder. Twice Sheylha's warning shout had saved him. Twice she had called him by name. And yet he had never told her what it was.

2

———

Pain engulfed his world. It blundered recklessly through his consciousness, competing for attention with the fever talk that inundated his head.

A voice was there, too, sometimes a murmur, sometimes comprehensible. It whispered soothingly. Occasionally it sang softly to him.

There were times when he could hear and think normally. Birds called in the forest, and the wind sighed in the treetops above. Before long he always slipped away again into blackness.

His past paraded itself before him, in all its aching beauty and excruciating agony. At times the torment of the memories eclipsed the physical pain. He saw again his bride, radiant and carefree, running to him with delight on her face. He saw his child, a perfect miniature of her mother, laughing as she played in the sunshine.

Through it all he watched as his brother turned away from their joy, anguish in his eyes. He felt himself shrugging helplessly once again. The decision had been neither his nor his brother's—she had made the choice.

He stumbled anew upon the murky trade in precious gems. He comprehended the risks, but could not ignore the dazzle of great reward. His wife's smile slowly faded as his secret hoard grew, but he willed himself not to notice. He told himself it was only temporary. Just until he could establish his fortune. Then he would leave it all behind.

But the greed had taken hold. The shadow of fear rarely left his wife's face now, though he no longer regarded it. His brother's bafflement did not move him—let his sibling remain a poor farmer if that made him content. Kalvor was destined for greater things.

His trade was perilous, and he soon controlled a network of ambitious, and often dangerous, men. He had become dangerous himself. He was not a man to be trifled with.

The business led him further from home. Long absences from his family became necessary and gradually ceased to trouble him. His wealth was growing rapidly. He kept telling himself that it wouldn't need to be for much longer.

And then it had all come crashing down.

He had returned home one day, calling for his wife and daughter, only to find their lifeless bodies sprawled on the ground. The two guards he had hired lay dead beside them. His hoard was bare—all of it gone. The robbers had surely forced the location of the hiding place from his wife. She would have volunteered it readily—she cared nothing for the money. Nevertheless, they had not been gentle with her.

Faced with the horrific consequences of his priorities, he understood too late the magnitude of his own folly.

He wasn't the only one who had loved his wife. His brother had loved her hopelessly from a distance, and Kalvor could not face him. Surely his sibling must hate him with a bitter passion. Kalvor became restless and agitated. He had to do something.

Grief had quickly turned to rage. He paused long enough to bury them, then he abandoned his trade and set out for revenge. It had taken many months to trace each of the killers, but he was singleminded. One by one he tracked them down and exacted payment from them in kind—blood for blood.

When it was finally over, he found himself restless and dissatisfied still. The aching void remained, and he had no idea where to turn.

He was offered a task to occupy him—the opportunity to avenge an acquaintance. Retribution was well deserved, and the job paid handsomely. He discovered he was good at it. Others soon heard of his capabilities and sought him out. One step at a time, and without conscious intent, he gradually underwent a transformation. He had always been tall and strong and relentless. Now he became an object of terror—a hired assassin, a killer without remorse. He wasn't above abductions if the fee was right.

None of it numbed the pain of his loss. In time he learned to force it out of his awareness, to push it far away where he had no need to deal with it.

THE VOICE SPOKE AGAIN in his memory. *He never hated you.* The voice was familiar to him now. *Your brother. He never hated you.*

He hadn't turned to his brother in his grief. Perhaps everything might have been different if he had.

But what did it matter? Even if his brother had somehow found it within him to offer comfort and support, Kalvor knew that his own stubbornness and pride would never have allowed him to receive it. Such support was entirely unearned and undeserved.

And it could never have satisfied him. His debt was too great to be so easily discharged. His wife and daughter had paid the ultimate price for his greed. There was no opportunity now to cast himself down before them and beg for their forgiveness. Where could he possibly turn for absolution?

Silent tears made tracks across his cheeks as he slid again into the blessed release of nothingness.

THE WOMAN—SHEYLHA—KNELT before a small fire, humming quietly to herself. He drank in the sight of her.

Turning in his direction, she noticed his attention and greeted him with a smile. "Welcome, Kalvor. So you have decided to rejoin the living?"

He did not try to speak. Her quiet movements captivated him, and he contented himself with watching her. She gazed at him for a long moment, a thoughtful look on her face. Then she turned aside, away from the intensity in his eyes, and continued with her chores.

He was too weary to watch for long. Sleep soon claimed him once more.

"Why?" It was the first word he had spoken, and all he could manage.

Nothing further was needed—she understood. "Why not?" she replied. "Do you think you weren't worth saving?"

He didn't respond. He just lay there, watching her and waiting.

"I had hope for you. In spite of everything." She regarded him frankly. "I had to dig deep to find it."

She softened her words with a smile. Approaching him, she examined his bandages, tending him with gentle and skillful fingers. It was hard to imagine a more considerate nurse—she seemed to sense what caused him pain the same moment he became aware of it.

"How?"

"How do I know things?" Her face clouded over for a moment. "You're not ready to hear that. Not now. Maybe not ever."

He wasn't offended in the least. He wasn't even sure if it was possible for her to offend him.

She sighed. Then she adopted a detached air. "We need meat. I'm going outside to check the traps. As for you, the thing you need to concentrate on is getting well again."

The day came when Kalvor was able to walk again. His injuries were not fully healed, but he was impatient to get back on his feet.

The weather was closing in, and decisions needed to be made while there was still time.

"I can build a shelter for the winter. I'll need to find the right place."

She nodded her agreement. "You can decide the location."

The next couple of weeks were hard work. He found a secluded site within the borders of Arvenon. It was deep within the forest, not far from a stream, and sheltered from the worst of the weather. Tall trees surrounded it on all sides, making it unlikely that smoke from their fire would be easy to detect.

It took him much longer to build the shelter than he expected. His recovering body still limited him frustratingly. With few tools at hand and restricted time he kept it simple. He managed to fashion a crude chimney, though, and gather a large pile of wood. They moved into the shelter before it began to snow in earnest.

He had abandoned any thought of his original mission. There was no longer any question of taking her to Lord Drettroth. Nor was there a need to inform her about the change in his intentions—she knew such things without needing to be told.

He asked a question that had long been on his mind. "The village in Lestanor—why did you need to leave it?"

"Those men you fought—they were sent by a person who believed he owned the entire region. Me included. You weren't the first person attacked by his thugs. None of the others gave back as good as they got, though. Not like you did.

"He was becoming very demanding. He wanted to use me to manipulate others. It would have ended badly—for me and for people I cared about."

"I'm not going to let anyone hurt you." His tone was matter-of-fact, but a resolve as unyielding as granite lay behind the words.

He had always needed a purpose in life—it had been true since he was a small child. His purpose now was to protect this woman. He owed it to her, and he had never been one to leave his debts unpaid.

She eyed him with a raised eyebrow. "You're in no state to fight anyone."

He shrugged. "Fighting doesn't seem to be necessary right now."

She laughed, a merry sound. "May it long continue to be true."

. . .

THE TWO OF them quickly became comfortable in each other's company. Kalvor could not complain about someone so understanding and accepting of his needs and his moods. For Sheylha's part, she seemed to very much appreciate a break from dealing with demanding people.

Kalvor was a man of few words, but Sheylha didn't seem to mind. He had long since accepted that she knew what he was thinking, so he saw little need to speak anyway. She somehow seemed able to reach into his mind to see his past, too. He wasn't entirely sure how he felt about that, but he trusted her completely. And he hadn't forgotten how much he owed her.

SHEYLHA'S favorite meal was fresh fish, and she never tired of idling away a few stray hours angling with a pole. Downstream, not far from their shelter, she had found a location frequented by trout. Kalvor often joined her there to fish. Whenever they enjoyed success they would squat together beside the stream to clean their catch, then they would return to the shelter and poach the fish in a pan over the fire.

With the onset of winter, the stream began to freeze over. Arriving one day at their favorite spot with hopes of fresh fish for dinner, they found it covered with ice. Before Kalvor could protest, Sheylha grabbed a fallen branch and stepped nimbly out onto the frozen surface of the stream. Alarmed at the risk she was taking, he called a warning.

"Don't worry! I've done this before," she called back cheerily.

Standing on the thicker ice near the bank, she began energetically laying into the ice around their fishing hole with the branch. He considered following her, but quickly decided that it would simply increase the risk of disaster.

The ice resisted at first, but soon began to splinter steadily under her blows. In a few short minutes she had almost cleared the fishing hole. She paused to rest.

An ominous cracking sound shattered the stillness.

"Get out of there!"

His cry of alarm came too late. The ice beneath her broke into pieces, and she was pitched headlong into the freezing water. The stream was not deep, and she pulled herself to her feet, shivering with the cold as icy water poured off her.

A broad sheet of ice still clung to the bank, preventing Kalvor from reaching her. She clambered onto the ice, trying to escape the stream. Her weight was more than the ice could bear, though, and a new piece broke away, dumping her back into the water. She struggled upright again, beginning to show signs of exhaustion.

Kalvor found a fallen branch and passed one end to her. She grasped hold of it, and he began to pull her in. Before she made it all the way across the remaining ice, though, her nerveless fingers lost their grip, and she slipped back into the water.

He grabbed a lump of wood and smashed away the ice that remained between Sheylha and the bank.

"Come to me," he called urgently.

She somehow found her feet once again and lurched forward. Stumbling suddenly upon something underfoot, she pitched forward into the water. This time she did not manage to stand upright again.

She had done enough, though. Kalvor grabbed hold of her clothing and dragged her out of the river by main force.

She was utterly spent. There was no question of her walking back to the shelter. He positioned himself in front of her, facing away. Kneeling down, he pulled her arms over his shoulders, clasping them tightly across his chest. Then he stood upright, lifting her with him, and set off for home.

By the time he reached the shelter he was soaking wet as well, and shivering with the cold. She was blue and barely seemed to be breathing. He stripped off her clothes, then tore off his own, letting the sodden garments lie where they fell. Then he dragged her into the warm shelter.

Grabbing a pile of furs, he spread them out before the fire, then lay down shivering on top of them before reaching for her, drawing her close to allow her body to absorb his own warmth. He shuddered with the shock as her icy cold body came into contact with his own. Covering them both with furs, he settled down to wait.

Eventually he slipped into an exhausted slumber. When he woke his own body temperature felt more normal. Some color had returned to her face as well. Locating some of her dry clothing, he pulled it onto her before settling her once again.

She slept through the hours of darkness without waking. He spent a tense night at her side, constantly checking her condition.

By the time the dawn came she was burning up with fever.

Thoroughly alarmed, he set out on a desperate hunt for feverwort, searching everywhere for any glimpse of its broad leaf and white flower. Feverwort was almost certainly growing somewhere nearby, but snow covered the ground, and he could find no sign of it.

He had no idea what to do, apart from trying to get her to swallow fluids.

As the day wore on her condition worsened. For the first time he began to fear that he might lose her. He couldn't bring himself to face even the possibility of such an outcome.

He went outside the shelter and cried aloud to the heavens, beseeching the mercy of the Dark Gods of Rogand—Malzakh the Destroyer and his fearsome sister, Nehrvina the Awful. He didn't doubt that turning to them for compassion was an exercise in futility, though, and he was soon casting about elsewhere in his search for hope. Sheylha had a softness for the god of Arvenon, and Kalvor tried to recall anything he'd heard about him. This deity had supposedly sacrificed himself for the sake of mortals. It sounded implausible, but he sent an earnest plea in his direction anyway. He would have pleaded with the gods of Lestanor, too, if he'd known anything of substance about them.

Sheylha clung to life throughout another sleepless night for Kalvor. She lingered on through the following day, then as the sun began to set, her fever finally broke.

By the morning she had opened her eyes. He trembled as he gazed at her, not certain if his unsteadiness was due to relief or fatigue. He fed her a vegetable broth he had prepared, and she managed to swallow some of it. Her dull eyes soon closed, though, and she slept.

Exhaustion overtook him, and he finally succumbed to sleep himself. When he eventually woke he discovered that he had slept through the entire day and the following night.

She lay silent among the furs, watching him. He leaped up, guilty at leaving her untended for so long.

"My clothes," she asked weakly. "Where are they?"

"You needn't worry—nothing happened," he assured her.

He immediately felt foolish. She, of all people, didn't need to be told such things.

"That isn't what I meant," she said. "I need the clothes I was wearing." She sounded surprisingly anxious.

He looked at her curiously. He didn't understand her request at all. "They're outside," he told her. "I can get them if you like."

"Please," she said simply, nodding.

He went outside and rummaged around in the snow until he found her garments. After brushing off as much loose snow as he could, he brought them inside.

"Could you please look away?"

That surprised him even more, but he complied with her request.

She went quiet for a time as she handled her garments. Then she spoke again. "Thank you." She sounded enormously relieved.

"You can look again now."

He turned back to her.

"I don't need these anymore." She was offering him all of the clothing except one undergarment. He regarded her with a puzzled frown, then he shrugged and took the clothes. He hung them inside in a place where they would eventually dry out.

Before the sun had set she was on her feet again.

By the time a couple more days had passed she seemed almost back to normal.

3

———————

Outwardly life had resumed its normal rhythm. The reality, though, was that nothing could ever be the same again for either of them.

Kalvor looked back on their early weeks together as a time of innocence that had vanished forever. Sheylha's near death experience had stirred up intense emotions in him, and having suppressed his emotions for so long, he had no idea how to deal with them now.

Almost losing Sheylha had shaken Kalvor to the core. Crippling fear had gripped him as he watched her teeter on the brink of death. He had actually pleaded with the gods, an act he never imagined himself capable of.

He had kept her alive by lying with her skin to skin. There had been nothing sexual—much less romantic—about the experience. Nevertheless, it had awakened something in him. He had become aware of a hollow void within himself, and a nagging hunger for something more. He no longer knew how to be natural around her.

It hadn't previously bothered him that she knew his thoughts and his emotions, but now he felt exposed and uncomfortable. For the first time he wished he had similar insights into her.

He could have simply asked her what she was thinking and feeling, of course. But she knew what was on his mind, and she could have volunteered answers if she'd wanted to.

Once or twice he noticed her reaching out tentatively, as if to comfort him. But she had quickly withdrawn her hand and turned away.

They seemed to have reached an impasse, with neither of them willing to take the risk of crossing the divide.

Kalvor was out checking his traps when he was startled into alertness by a nearby sound. He looked up to find himself staring into an unfamiliar face. Instinctively he adopted a fighting stance. The stranger, who wore the robes of a monk, assessed Kalvor calmly, ignoring the implied threat.

With the monk showing no signs of aggression, Kalvor willed himself to relax. As he studied the cleric, an idea began to form in his mind. "Come with me, if you are willing," he said. "You will be welcome in our humble shelter. Please share a meal with us."

At the mention of food, the monk brightened visibly, readily accepting his invitation.

Sheylha was delighted to see the monk, and Kalvor busied himself preparing a meal while they conversed. As he worked, he consciously cleared his mind of anything apart from the task at hand.

Conversation between Sheylha and the visitor continued unabated throughout the meal. When all of them had finally satisfied their hunger, the monk sat back with a contented sigh.

Kalvor began watching Sheylha intently. The moment she glanced across at him, he locked eyes with her and opened himself to her probing. Her eyes widened. A deep blush covered her face as she read the question in his eyes. She sat unmoving for a long, lingering moment, then inclined her head, so slightly it was almost imperceptible. It was enough for him.

He turned to the monk. "I hope you enjoyed the meal."

"I did," the cleric confirmed. "Very much indeed."

"Would you be willing to do us a small favor in return?"

"Gladly, if it is within my power."

"Would you please marry us?"

THE MONK HAD GONE after pronouncing a blessing over them and their household. Having seen him off, Kalvor returned to the shelter and stepped inside.

Sheylha had arranged a bed of furs and laid herself down upon them. He offered her his thoughts without reserve, knowing that none of his hopes and dreams were hidden from her. She reached for him once more, and this time she did not draw back.

BY THE TIME winter had passed, Kalvor had recovered from his injuries. He scouted widely around their dwelling in every direction, and saw no sign that their refuge had been detected. Nor could he see any obvious reason why it might be detected in the future.

Kalvor's wounds might have healed, but he had yet to regain his full strength. In particular, he began to work hard to recapture his fighting edge. Sheylha always seemed willing to pause to admire her new husband as he put himself through his paces. Beyond that, she seemed content enough to spend the bulk of her time working away at the necessary chores of life.

He had a number of questions. He tried not to overwhelm her with them, though.

"Why did you agree to go with me in the village in Lestanor? You knew what I was intending to do."

"Yes, I knew," she agreed. "But I also saw things in you that you weren't able to see for yourself. You may not have realized it, but you were ripe for change. You just needed a nudge."

He wasn't sure what to say. He always needed time to absorb her revelations. She seemed to be in an answering mood, though, so he continued with another of his questions.

"Your gift—is that how you healed my wounds?"

She shook her head. "No. I can't use it to heal physical wounds. It helps, though, because I can see when someone is in pain. And when I'm tending wounds, I know if my actions are making the pain better or worse."

"You're the most gentle nurse I've ever known."

She smiled. She seemed to ponder for a long moment before continuing. Then her face became serious. "I think you're aware that I can see into the minds of other people," she told him. "That has the potential to be a very dangerous gift."

He simply nodded. Some people would stop at nothing to control such an ability.

"It reveals the past to you as well, doesn't it?" he said.

"Yes," she agreed. "You have seen evidence of that.

"At first I didn't know what to do with this gift," she told him. "I was terrified of it. Then I became inquisitive about people. I couldn't help myself—I pried into everything. It became very empty. Eventually I decided I would try to use the knowledge for good. I wanted to do whatever I could to heal people."

"But you said you can't heal wounds."

"I don't mean physical wounds. Many people are deeply wounded in their spirits. They can't easily see the roots of their own problems. With careful study, I usually can."

"So you saw that my brother's attitude was important to me. How could you be sure that he never hated me, though? You couldn't see into his mind, could you?"

"No, I couldn't. But I was able to witness your interactions with him, hidden away deep in your memory. Your conscious memory doesn't take you back that far anymore. At the time you agonized over what had happened, and you came to some conclusions about what your brother was thinking. Those conclusions are what you remember now. I was able to see these conclusions, as well as what originally took place between you and your brother. It became clear to me that your brother's attitude wasn't quite how you interpreted it."

"So I was about to take away your freedom and put your life in danger, and you were thinking about my brother?"

She shrugged. "I'm well acquainted with being in danger. And I've learned not to worry too much about the future. I'm no use to anyone, myself included, if I give in to that."

He gazed at her with renewed respect. Very few people seemed even vaguely capable of looking beyond their own self interest.

"So it somehow helps people if they learn to see their own past differently?"

She nodded. "People tell themselves things that aren't true. Setting it straight often changes them."

All this seemed like a foreign language to him. But apparently it made sense to her. "Are you sorry that you're not helping people anymore?"

She sighed. "It had become very tiring. I am grateful for a rest from it—a long rest."

He could see the point of helping others from time to time—even strangers. But people constantly coming at you, expecting you to somehow fix them? It would have driven him mad. "How many people came to see you?"

"I never counted. But it must have been hundreds."

He shook his head. She must have seemed a god-like figure to them. "I imagine they miss you."

"I'm sure that most of the common people miss me. They were grateful for my help, and they repaid me with love and respect. But others—too many others—lusted after my gift. Keeping them at bay became a constant struggle. I found it more and more exhausting. It's such a relief to be free of it."

It was very clear to him that she had badly needed to escape from the expectations and the strife. In time she might begin to miss it, though. "Do you think you will ever want to return to that life?"

"I don't know. It's hard to imagine hiding away for the rest of my days when there's so much need in the world. Perhaps if you were there to help me I could find a way to make it work. I'm in no hurry, though."

He sat silently, pondering all she had told him. To a stranger, the picture she had been painting would have seemed like no more than the ravings of a lunatic. But he had seen for himself the power and impact of her gifts.

"I've been very careful with what I say about this," she told him frankly. "No one else understands the full extent of what I'm able to see and do."

"Why are you willing to trust me with this information?"

She smiled, although there was no humor in it. "Remember that I can see into your mind. I trust you because I understand your intent. Perhaps better than you do."

THEY HAD CARVED out a simple but idyllic existence for themselves in the wilderness. More than three years had passed since Kalvor first built their shelter, and a sturdy cabin had taken its place. Three of them shared the cabin now—their daughter Ahnya was the delight of their lives, and she had just turned two.

They were acutely aware that nothing lasts forever, though.

The first hint of trouble came when Kalvor spotted a Rogandan soldier making his way stealthily through the trees, less than a day's march from their dwelling. Instantly alert, he began thoroughly scouting the whole region. Before he returned to report his discovery to his wife, he had established beyond doubt that the soldier was just one of many.

"We need to leave. Now." Kalvor moved quickly around the cabin, selectively choosing a few items and stuffing them into a sack.

Dismay showed clearly on Sheylha's face. "Are you sure this is necessary, Kal? They might not be looking for us."

"These are Drettroth's men, and they're searching for us. They're led by a man called Marek. I know him—he hasn't come here for a chat." He knew she could uncover the truth for herself in his mind, but saying it out loud somehow made it more solid.

"It must have been the monk," he said bitterly.

She opened her mouth to protest, but he forestalled her. "I don't mean he exposed us intentionally. It probably made a great fireside story—the monk stumbles upon a couple living together in the forest in unlikely innocence; he provides them with their happy ending. No one would forget such a tale."

He threw up his hands in frustration. "We should have moved. Far away from here."

Kalvor turned aside, moving quickly about the cabin. As soon as he had gathered a few essential supplies, he spoke to Sheylha urgently. "I have some preparations I need to make. I'll be gone, perhaps for an hour. Be ready to leave the moment I return." Then he vanished among the trees.

Sheylha was ready when he returned. She was only leaving with great reluctance, but she accepted it.

He led them rapidly away from their home. "We're heading to Arnost. The capital of the kingdom of Arvenon probably seems like an unlikely place to hide, so maybe they won't be expecting it. Either way, it's probably as good a destination as any when a large group of Rogandan soldiers is on your trail."

Just before nightfall he found a secluded spot for them to rest. "I'm going to do some hunting of my own. I'll be back before dawn. If I don't make it back by mid morning for any reason, keep heading west until you come to a main road. It leads to Arnost. Try to join a group of other travelers if you can."

She couldn't hide her anxiety. He ignored it. He lifted up their daughter and hugged her briefly before kissing Sheylha gently on the lips. Then he was gone.

He returned as dawn was breaking. Ahnya greeted him with a glad cry and he scooped her into his arms.

Sheylha could not contain her joy and relief at seeing him. She looked tired—he hadn't slept that night, and she probably hadn't, either.

He tried to cloud his mind. "Don't try to see my thoughts," he warned her. "You might find some distressing images there."

She snatched her eyes away.

"It's enough to say that I've long prepared against the possibility of this day. I had a warm welcome ready for them, and they didn't miss any of it. While they were distracted I took the opportunity to further reduce their numbers." He hung his head. "There are so many of them, though. They torched the cabin. I couldn't prevent it."

He hardened himself—he had a wife and child to consider. Not for the first time. This time he would not abandon his family for any reason. "I left a false trail to buy us some time."

For her sake, he put the images of death and confusion from his mind, and resolutely set his thoughts on the future. He picked up their daughter and shouldered his sack, then he led them forward.

4

————

Kalvor glanced up at the sun, then across at Sheylha. The day had barely begun and already both of them were bone-weary. Traveling on foot with a small child meant frustratingly slow progress, and once again he berated himself for failing to acquire horses during their period of isolation.

In the hope of making up time, the little group made their way onto the main road. Noticing a caravan behind them traveling in the same direction, they paused to consider their options.

"Perhaps we should join them for a while," Sheylha suggested.

Kalvor didn't answer immediately. It would benefit them enormously if they could catch a ride. But they had no money to barter with, and exposing themselves would involve enormous risks.

The urgency of picking up the pace finally decided him. "Very well," he said reluctantly. "But not for long. And only while they're moving forward. We'll need to leave the minute they stop."

They quickly discovered that the caravan consisted of several Rogandan trading families. The traders readily welcomed Kalvor and his little family into their midst, and they soon found themselves riding on an open wagon in the middle of the column.

The bustle and noise of a caravan made for a dizzying change after the peace and quiet of the forest. Sheylha seemed to adjust immediately to the breathless pace of human interaction. Kalvor set his jaw and tried not to be noticed.

"What's your daughter's name? And how old is she?" asked one of the women.

"Her name is Ahnya," Sheylha replied with a smile. "She's two."

"She's so good at talking!"

It was true—Sheylha had assured him that Ahnya was unusually advanced. But how many children had a mother who always knew exactly what they were trying to communicate—a mother instantly able to help them find the right word?

"I see you have a little one too," Sheylha returned, nodding toward a screaming baby. "Is he unwell?"

"He's very unsettled. I simply can't understand what's wrong with him—it's so hard when they're too young to tell you."

"May I hold him?"

"Of course." The mother nodded to her older daughter, and she handed over the squawking infant.

Sheylha examined him silently for a couple of minutes. Then she tilted him this way and that before patting him firmly on the back a few times, first in one location, then in another. Several loud burps sounded, and the baby stopped crying.

The other woman looked at Sheylha with awe in her eyes. "Thank you! You're amazing! Do you know what makes him so upset?"

"It seems to be wind," she said, handing him back. "After each feed it might be helpful to spend some time getting rid of it."

"But I do! I've always burped my babies, but it's never seemed to fix the problem with him. I thought it was severe colic—or something much worse."

Sheylha smiled. "It's nothing serious. He just seems to be a lot more windy than your others were."

"How do you know so much about babies?"

She smiled again. "I've had some experience with them."

The conversation continued to flow without pause. Kalvor kept his head down, successfully managing to avoid attention.

The day had almost worn away by the time the wagons eventually came to a halt.

"Come and camp near us tonight," the woman suggested eagerly. "The caravan is going to pause for a couple of days before pushing on to Arnost."

Sheylha looked at Kalvor hopefully.

"We need to keep moving," he said regretfully, forcing a smile. "We're eager to reach Arnost as soon as possible."

"That's a shame. Happy travels, then. Thank you so much for your help with my baby!"

They said their farewells, and hurried off.

"We couldn't have stayed for one night?"

He shook his head firmly. "If Drettroth's men found us, the traders couldn't have protected us. We needed to leave quickly. The men pursuing us will discover soon enough that we've been there."

They hurried along the road for a couple of hours after the sun disappeared below the horizon. Then they sought out a suitable location among the trees, well away from the road. They settled down to spend the night there.

"Just one more day of travel, and we should be in Arnost," he told her.

They were silent for a time, not speaking again until their daughter had drifted off to sleep.

"Kal, there's something I need to tell you."

He peered at her curiously.

"I've never told you where my gift came from."

"You were born with it, weren't you?"

"No. It isn't what you think. It isn't an ability I inherited at birth. All of the insight comes from a very simple source—just a small stone. It's colorful and attractive, but there isn't much else that's remarkable about it. And yet it allows me to see the thoughts of other people."

He looked at her in surprise. "A stone? Where did you get it from?"

"I found it when I was a young woman living in Lestanor. I was fishing, and I noticed it lying at the bottom of the stream. It was catching the sunlight. It looked attractive, so I waded in and picked it up.

"I have no idea how it came to be there. I haven't been able to learn anything at all about its origins or why it behaves as it does. It's a great mystery. It took me a very long time before I fully discovered what it was capable of."

"So this stone lets you see what a person is thinking? Any person?"

"It's only effective when I look at someone. And I have to be holding the stone at the time."

He gazed at her in puzzlement. "But you don't walk around all day holding a stone."

"No. I sewed it into one of my undergarments in such a way that it stays constantly in contact with my skin."

He frowned, trying to make sense of what she was telling him.

"After I nearly died of the cold after falling in the stream, do you remember that I asked you to bring me my clothes? I was anxious to get the undergarment that held the stone. I almost never take it off."

"Except when we're intimate."

A delicate blush covered her face. "That's true. There are times when I don't need distractions. I don't always want to be different. I want to be a normal woman, too—to have the same feelings and experiences as every other woman."

He looked into her eyes tenderly, filled with amazement once again that she had chosen him.

An intense look came across her face. "What I'm trying to tell you is that the stone's powers are not restricted to me. If someone else possesses the stone, they will receive all of these abilities with it."

Kalvor went cold inside. He was beginning to understand for the first time why Lord Drettroth had been so eager to have the seer in his clutches. "Drettroth made a strange comment," he recalled. "I didn't understand it at the time, but it's starting to make sense now."

"What did he say?" she asked.

"He said that hearing about you and your powers made him remember something he'd once seen in an old scroll. He said he needed to do more research, but he seemed very excited.

"I took no notice of it. He wanted a job done, he'd always paid well, and that's all I cared about."

"So he was never planning to manipulate other people through me," said Sheylha. "He'd heard of the stone and wanted to try it out for himself." She shook her head, frowning.

Kalvor shuddered involuntarily. "Drettroth mustn't be allowed to get his hands on it!"

"I've removed it from my clothing," she told him. "You're stronger than I am. In the morning when we set off again I'm going to ask you to take care of it."

"Will I be able to see into your thoughts when I'm holding it?"

She shook her head. "Not while it still belongs to me. It doesn't seem to work like that."

She took his hands and gazed earnestly into his eyes. "If anything happens to me, promise me you will hide the stone where it will never be found. I don't need to tell you what will happen if it falls into the hands of someone who will misuse its power. It's better that no one has it. Promise me!" she insisted.

"I promise."

He wanted to reassure her—to tell her that he would protect her, that he wouldn't allow anything bad to happen to her. But the words stuck in his throat. How could he give her such assurances when the future was not within his control?

Neither of them slept that night.

They set out before dawn, hurrying along the road toward the Arvenian capital. True to her word, she had given him the stone. It sat securely in the leather pouch at his belt.

He drove them forward relentlessly. Something told him they could not afford to delay even for a moment.

. . .

THE CITY WAS in sight when they first caught a distant glimpse of horsemen behind them. Kalvor felt certain it was the Rogandans pursuing them. The gray stone towers of Arnost's castle were still far away, but they seemed to beckon, calling them to the safety of the walls that surrounded the city. They only needed to get to the river, cross the ford, and follow the road that wound its way through the foothills to the city gates. But they were on foot, and Drettroth's men were mounted.

"We're not going to reach Arnost in time," he said.

"Can't we hide in the forest?"

He shook his head. "They'll track us, and sooner or later they'll find us. On my own I might stand a chance, but not with the three of us. There are too many of them."

They were out of options. "We have to separate," he said. "It will be too easy for them if we stay together. You need to get Ahnya to safety!"

Tears filled her eyes, but she didn't argue.

"Take what's left of the food," he said, thrusting a small sack into her hand. "If I'm killed, stay hidden until they're gone. Then go far away from here. Search out a place where no one will find you—a place where Ahnya won't come to any harm."

She embraced him desperately. "I love you," she told him. "Thank you for three shining years."

He opened his thoughts to her, then abruptly remembered that she no longer had the stone. "You gave me back my life," he told her, "and you taught me how to truly love. Thank you!"

He reached down for Ahnya and drew her in close, rocking her back and forth.

The distant pursuers disappeared in a dip in the road. Kalvor pointed to a nearby slope covered with bushes, on the opposite side of the road to the forest. "You need to go! Up there! Get among the bushes and hide on the far side of the slope. You'll still be able to see the road. Hurry! I'll lead them away."

"But there are so many of them!"

"Let me worry about that."

"What about the stone? We need to hide it!"

"I'll dispose of it, right now. Before I do anything else. Whatever happens, keep our daughter safe! Don't come back down unless I call you. Promise me!"

After a moment's hesitation she returned a reluctant nod.

She reached out for their daughter. "Daddy, Daddy!" Ahnya cried, protesting tearfully as he handed her over. Kalvor kissed her tenderly on the forehead, hardening himself against the tears that rolled down his cheeks. He needed to be strong.

Sheylha bundled Ahnya into her arms and shouldered the sack with the food. Then she hurried off across the slope. She was fit and lean, and he soon lost sight of her among the foliage.

Kalvor looked back for any sign of the hunters. They were still out of sight. Now was the perfect moment to make good his promise about the stone.

Finding a place beside the road where the soil was soft, he used his knife to quickly dig a deep hole. Then he lifted the stone from his pouch and cast it in. Finally he filled the hole, scooping loose soil and stones over it until it was covered. Only a close examination would reveal any disturbance now.

If they all somehow made it to safety, they could come back for the stone later.

He stood up quickly and looked around. A quick scan of the surrounding area revealed no easily defensible location. Ahead of him the road was bisected by a river. He sprinted along the road until he reached the ford. Hurrying to the crossing, he waded quickly across the river and raced up the opposite bank to rejoin the road.

Beyond the river the road bent around in a broad sweep, and he hastened along it. A short distance ahead he spotted a rocky outcrop beside the road. It might offer a defensible position. He was an archer without peer—he would pick them off with arrows from behind cover.

The outcrop lay on the same side of the road as Sheylha's hiding place. She would be able to observe him from across the river.

The odds were stacked against him, but he would not sell himself cheaply. He cared only about drawing Drettroth's men away from his wife and daughter. And denying Drettroth the stone.

As he hurried forward, he glanced back over his shoulder. He caught a brief glimpse of his pursuers before the bend hid them from view. It would take no more than a few minutes before they reached the ford.

He ran until he was gasping for air, inhaling ragged breaths into heaving lungs. When he reached the outcrop he stole a glance behind and saw his pursuers crossing the river. Hastily he began laying out his arrows. He had at least thirty shafts. He intended to make them count.

The hunters rounded the bend at full gallop. He reacted without conscious effort, taking rapid aim with his bow and releasing arrows.

Marek had been riding hard, followed closely by the twenty of his men who remained. If the traders in the caravan were to be believed, Kalvor was traveling not only with a woman—presumably the seer— but with their child. He spat. The hunter had gone soft.

A self-satisfied smirk covered his face when he caught a distant glimpse of two people on the road ahead. They were apparently heading in the direction of Arnost. They might try to hide in the forest, but if they did they'd be wasting their energy. It was only a matter of time now.

The fugitives were still far away, but his men were mounted and closing fast. The road dipped and for several minutes Marek lost sight of them entirely. As the terrain rose again he caught a brief glimpse of Kalvor before the warrior disappeared around a bend in the road. Even at a distance Marek recognized his huge frame.

The horses splashed across the ford and surged up the other side. When they rounded the bend in the road, no one was in sight. Then arrows flew toward them, and several of his men tumbled from the saddle. Marek belatedly spotted Kalvor, positioned behind some rocks.

He snorted. The renegade might have taken the searchers by surprise earlier among the trees, but not even Kalvor could overcome twenty men in the open without support.

Marek shouted instructions. Two of his men rode on toward Arnost, searching for the woman with her child.

The archers among them drew their bows and began to return the fire.

SHEYLHA WATCHED ANXIOUSLY from her hiding place on the ridge as their pursuers galloped past, entirely unaware of her presence above them. Having seen them, cold sweat broke out across her brow, and her heart began to pound. How could Kalvor possibly defeat so many?

If Drettroth's men succeeded in killing him they would begin searching for her next. Even if they caught her, though, she wouldn't be able to tell them where the stone was hidden. She hadn't actually seen Kalvor dispose of it, but she didn't doubt for a moment that he had fulfilled his promise. It wouldn't find its way into Drettroth's clutches.

Kalvor had seen the mounted men now, and he was firing arrows at them. Several of the men fell, but the rest quickly surrounded him. Her heart beat faster.

They were firing arrows back, but they didn't seem able to bring him down. Instead it was the attackers who were falling, one at a time.

Kalvor had single-handedly taken on an overwhelming force. Her eyes grew wider as she watched him gradually bring it down to size. It was only with great effort that she prevented herself from leaping to her feet and cheering out loud.

5

An arrow struck the rock beside Kalvor's head and skidded past his cheek, drawing blood. There was no point trying to dodge the arrows—they were coming in too fast. But he had chosen his location well. He could only trust to luck or providence now.

More of his arrows were finding their mark. He could see the frustration growing among his opponents. None of their archers were skillful enough to hit a partially protected target while shooting from horseback. And it wouldn't be helping their concentration to see men steadily falling all around them.

At first he targeted the bowmen. Then he realized that after the last archer was gone, the survivors would rush him. He couldn't hold all of them off. So he kept at the bowmen until just two of them remained, then he began picking off the others.

Marek was too canny to make himself an easy target. He hung back, contenting himself with yelling orders at the others. And he never stayed in one location for more than a moment.

The ground was littered with bodies now. Kalvor could see only Marek and three others still facing him. He had even managed to retrieve a couple of spent arrows they'd fired at him. For the first time he dared to hope.

———

MAREK GROUND his teeth in frustration as more of his men went down. He had expected his archers to finish it quickly, but they were worthless.

He knew of Kalvor's reputation, but until now he had never seen the man in action. He called down a bitter curse on the tall bowman.

Marek's options were diminishing rapidly, along with the men remaining to him. It had begun to dawn on him that Kalvor had chosen his location well. The bowman was taking full advantage of the only available cover, while his men were reduced to attacking in the open. He wondered briefly if Kalvor might have used a different strategy if he'd been leading the attack. He thrust such self doubts aside, screaming his frustration instead at the few men who remained.

The situation had become increasingly dire when a shaft caught Kalvor in the shoulder. The rain of arrows from the outcrop ceased instantly.

Seizing his opportunity, Marek spurred his horse in close, leaping off its back with his sword drawn.

His rival saw him coming. Gritting his teeth, he reached down for his own sword, struggling to draw it out. As he stepped into the open to give himself room, another arrow took him in the thigh. He hit the ground hard, writhing in agony.

Everything had changed, so abruptly and so completely.

Marek strode up to Kalvor, gloating at the sight of the mighty warrior lying prostrate and completely helpless before him. The renegade had caused him far too much trouble and accounted for far too many of his men. How could Marek possibly explain to Lord Drettroth that one man had taken out almost his entire squad? Lusting to repay the humiliation, he planted his foot on Kalvor's neck and ground his face into the dirt.

"Where's the seer?" he snarled.

"Somewhere you'll never find her," Kalvor gasped.

"Wrong answer, scum!" Marek reached down and twisted the arrow protruding from Kalvor's shoulder. His victim appeared to black out momentarily from the pain.

Marek kept enough pressure on Kalvor's neck that he could barely breathe. But the fool still had something to say. "Tell Drettroth," he wheezed, "he'll never find what he's looking for. She got rid of it. It wasn't worth the trouble."

With no useful answers on offer, Marek lost patience. He wasn't given to subtlety. Plunging his sword into Kalvor's back, he ended the conversation permanently.

The warrior breathed out a final whispered sigh, "Sheylha..." Then his body went limp.

Marek looked down at him contemptuously.

"That's a relief," said one of the other survivors shakily.

"The job's not finished," Marek growled. "Not until we have the woman. Lord Drettroth said to bring Kalvor in dead, but he wanted the woman alive. We'll all be served up as meat for Malzakh if we go back without her."

The other three paled visibly. They knew as well as he did that Drettroth would not hesitate to execute them all if he was unhappy enough. And Malzakh the Destroyer would be waiting hungrily to devour them in the afterlife.

At that moment the two riders returned.

"She got away. Into Arnost," one of them reported.

Marek spat. "How do you know it was her?"

"It was a woman carrying a child," the other replied. "Just like the traders said. We saw her hurrying through the gates."

"Idiots!" Marek sneered. "There must be hundreds of women with children going through those gates every day. We have to search for her."

He pointed to Kalvor's body. "Bind him up so he won't stink," he ordered. "Any of his loose belongings go into this sack. We were told to bring everything back untouched."

They tightly wrapped Kalvor's body and secured it over a horse. Then they dug a shallow grave and buried their dead. There were a lot of bodies, and it took a long time.

As soon as they'd completed their labors Marek gathered them together. "We need to find the woman. There are still six of us," he said. "We'll split up and search in pairs." He pointed at two of the men. "You two go back across the ford. If she didn't follow Kalvor to this side of the river, she'll have hidden back in the forest. Ride for an hour and start searching there." He pointed at two others. "You go back across the river as well. As soon as you reach the outskirts of the forest you can start searching in it. The two of us will search on this side of the river. We'll head toward Arnost."

He glanced up at the sky. The sun had passed its zenith, but a few hours of daylight remained. "We'll meet back here just before sunset."

"What if we don't find her?" one of the men asked. "She could be anywhere." He jerked a thumb toward the body of Kalvor. "If we go back to Lord Drettroth with nothing but him, we'll end up the same way."

"He's right!" agreed one of the others. "Lord Drettroth isn't known to be a reasonable man."

"So what do you propose?" sneered Marek.

"Why go back at all? Let him think we were all killed."

"He wouldn't just leave it at that, you halfwit!" Marek replied mockingly. "We all know he's searching for something. Whatever it is, he'll think we took it. He'll have us hunted down like dogs."

The other men went quiet.

"Just do as I told you," he snarled. "Get going!"

The first four men mounted their horses and headed for the river.

When Sheylha saw Kalvor drop his bow, her heart skipped a beat. He moved to the side, and the outcrop hid him from view. She couldn't tell what was happening. Her gut twisted into a tight knot. The tension became unbearable.

Sheylha didn't want to watch, but she couldn't tear her eyes away. She clutched her daughter to her helplessly. Not until Drettroth's men dragged Kalvor into the open and tightly wrapped him, completely covering his head, did Sheylha acknowledge to herself that he was dead. Then the tears blinded her as she sobbed her grief.

Her daughter began to wail loudly, no doubt responding to her mother's distress. Shocked out of her self-absorption, Sheylha pulled the child in close, shushing her frantically and desperately trying to muffle her cries. She looked up anxiously, but the men across the river seemed not to have heard.

Ahnya was her priority now. Sheylha managed to calm her, and in spite of her own agitation she somehow continued to comfort the child.

They would begin searching for her soon. But there were so few of them left. If she could only keep Ahnya quiet, they might not find her.

She saw the men separate into pairs. She watched anxiously as four of them crossed to her side of the river, riding in her direction. But they passed below her without looking up. Two of them rode on into the distance, back the way they had originally come.

The other two came to a halt not far beyond her hiding place. Would they come over to her side of the road and start searching the bushy slopes where she was hiding? Or would they turn away and search the forest? She looked on with heart pounding as they turned their backs on her, heading into the forest which lay on the opposite side of the road.

About an hour later they reappeared. They peered furtively back toward the ford, then they rode off at a gallop, following the two who had ridden that way earlier.

A LITTLE BEFORE sundown Marek and his companion returned to the rocky outcrop after spending the afternoon searching fruitlessly in the direction of Arnost.

They lit a fire, and sat down to wait. The sun sank lower in the sky and darkness fell. The clouds cleared, revealing a dazzling display of stars.

The minutes slipped away with no sign of the other four searchers.

Marek sat fuming. "Where are they?" he growled.

The other man watched him without speaking for a moment. Then he shrugged. "They're not coming back," he said.

"What are you talking about?"

He shrugged again. "They're scared."

Marek struggled to master his fury. "I'll kill the cowards myself!"

He glared at the fire as it hissed and crackled.

"What are you going to do?" his companion asked.

"I'm going back to Drettroth, of course," Marek replied. "I wasn't exaggerating before. If I don't return, Drettroth will have me hunted down."

"What are you going to tell him?"

"I'll tell him that Kalvor killed all the others. And that we saw the seer escape into Arnost. I'll also tell him what Kalvor said—about her deciding to get rid of whatever it is he's searching for." It was his turn to shrug. "Then I'll take my chances."

"I'll come with you," the other replied.

"Let's not waste any more time then," said Marek. They kicked dirt onto the fire and mounted their horses. They towed the horse bearing Kalvor's body behind them as they rode away.

The horses of their dead companions they left to wander wherever they would.

THROUGHOUT THE AFTERNOON Sheylha had cuddled her daughter, soothing her whenever she became distressed. Whenever she wanted to get up and wander around, Sheylha had sung to her softly or played quiet games with her. For the most part Ahnya was a placid child, and Sheylha never had more reason to be grateful for it.

When the sun sank low in the sky they shared a little food from the sack and drank water from a skin. As soon as it became dark, Ahnya settled into Sheylha's lap and went to sleep.

Sheylha had focused all her attention on keeping her daughter quiet and occupied. Once the last of Drettroth's men had disappeared into the distance, that burden finally lifted. Then the reality of Kalvor's death came crashing back in on her. How could she go on without him? How could she explain his absence to their daughter?

Tears welled up once more to flood her eyes, and sobs wracked her body. Ahnya woke and began to wail, and this time Sheylha made no attempt to restrain her. The two of them gave themselves over to their distress and howled together into the dark.

Eventually the tears dried up. With considerable effort, Sheylha managed to regain her composure. She recognized that this was a time to put the past behind her and face the future.

Everything would need to be different now. She had given up the stone willingly, and she had no desire to find it again. She was a seer no longer. The minds of others would forever be closed to her. She must find a new purpose in life.

Where could she go? She had no idea. But an opportunity of some kind would surely present itself. She was not without skills, and she was fluent in the languages of Arvenon, Rogand, and Lestanor. She would change her name and her identity and search out a way to provide for herself while she raised their daughter.

All that mattered now was Ahnya—she was precious beyond words. And she provided Sheylha with the only remaining link to her beloved husband.

Her immediate concern was to leave before any of their enemies decided to come back.

She glanced into the sack. There was probably enough food left in there for a couple of days. Shouldering the sack, she set Ahnya securely on her hip and made her way carefully back down the slope in the dark.

She headed along the road to the ford, intending to refill her skin in the river. A soft nickering caught her attention. Turning aside she found a horse, saddled and bridled. The animal nuzzled her, leaning in appreciatively as she stroked its head.

The opportunity was too good to miss. She lifted her daughter onto the horse, then climbed up behind her. Clicking her tongue, she guided the animal back onto the road, heading away from Arnost.

The outskirts of the forest soon appeared on her left. She rode on for a while before turning off the road, guiding her horse carefully among the trees. She didn't stop until she came to a meadow in a small clearing beside a stream. The meadow was secluded and well away from the road.

Overcome with exhaustion, she stopped the horse. Sliding from its back, she lifted her daughter down and set her in the meadow to rest among the wildflowers. She removed the horse's bridle and replaced it with a halter she found in a saddlebag. Then she secured the halter to a branch. Finally she lifted off its saddle.

Sheylha sat down in the dark beside Ahnya to find that the child had already fallen into a weary slumber.

With no pressing tasks to perform, Sheylha took a deep breath and willed her body to relax.

For a time she closed her eyes, remembering Kal and honoring him for who he was. She had loved him from the moment he stepped into her hut in Lestanor, cold and dangerous and wounded in spirit. She relived again the process by which he had received healing and had learned to appreciate life and goodness again. She remembered his quiet strength, their simple life in the forest, and the joy they had found together.

Then she exhaled slowly—a long shuddering sigh that rose up from the depths of her being. It began with murmurs of partings and bitter endings, of anguish beyond expression. It ended with soft whispers of hope, of peace that passes understanding.

She stilled herself once more, gazing up at the dark sky and the stars, listening to the call of the night birds and the burble of the water. Then she lay down beside Ahnya and slept.

In the morning Sheylha woke to find Ahnya stirring. She led her daughter to the stream. They both drank deeply, and she refilled the skin. Then she saddled and bridled the horse and they climbed once more into the saddle.

Turning their backs on all they had known, mother and daughter set their faces toward the vastness of the unpredictable world. Then they rode forward together.

They were soon lost to any certain knowledge.

EPILOGUE

The days gave way to months, and the months to years, and the Stone of Knowing lay hidden where Kalvor had buried it. Not even the wind and the rain disturbed it in its resting place.

It remained untouched until a day dawned when a burrowing animal chanced to unearth it. The animal dug energetically, scattering soil and debris everywhere. Having completed its labors, the creature scurried away.

The stone remained where it had fallen, exposed to the world once more.

A breeze sprang up and polished it clean, sweeping away any speck of dirt bold enough to linger on its surface.

Dazzling, alluring, and freely available once more, the stone gleamed brightly in the morning light.

It lay there unknowing, unaware of its influence, yet ready to capture the wandering glance of a new wide-eyed and unsuspecting guardian.

The End

**The story begins anew in *The Stone of Knowing*
(*The Stone Cycle Book 1*)
by Allan N. Packer**

NOTE FROM THE AUTHOR

Thank you for reading *The Seer: A Prequel to The Stone of Knowing*—I hope you enjoyed it. Please consider leaving a review on Amazon for the benefit of other readers.

If you have already read *The Stone of Knowing (The Stone Cycle Book 1)* and *The Cost of Knowing (The Stone Cycle Book 2)*, I hope this novelette provided some interesting additional background to the behavior of the Stone of Knowing, as well as how it came to be where Thomas found it. The story continues in *The Stone of Authority (The Stone Cycle Book 3)*.

If you have not yet read *The Stone of Knowing (The Stone Cycle Book 1)* and the *Stone Cycle* books that follow it, the journey has barely begun. You can find these novels at Amazon's Kindle store. Outlines follow for each of them below.

To be kept up to date on new releases, sign up to my mailing list at allanpacker.com. New subscribers will receive an exclusive bonus novelette, available in ebook and audiobook format. The novelette, *The Rending: A Prequel to The Cost of Knowing*, is also described below.

A small stone creates big ripples

The untroubled world of young Thomas Stablehand is changed forever when he stumbles upon an unusual stone. With the thoughts and intents of others laid bare, he eagerly indulges his curiosity. But seeing into other minds isn't like Thomas expected. And troubles are only beginning.

When invaders attack the kingdom of Arvenon, Thomas has nowhere to turn except to his friend Will Prentis, a gifted and ambitious leader who has risen rapidly in the ranks of the king's army.

Will is fearless, and where he leads men follow. With the kingdom on the brink, Will leads a small band on a perilous quest to thwart the invaders. Fearing his secret will be exposed, and hoping to help prevent catastrophe, Thomas flees with them.

But dangerous enemies seek the stone for their own ends. As Will faces a relentless opponent whose true purpose remains hidden, Thomas must decide what price he's willing to pay to protect the stone and preserve the kingdom.

The ripples begin to make waves

Thomas Stablehand's life is not the only thing spinning out of control since he found the stone. Entire kingdoms are now in turmoil.

Will Prentis, newly appointed as army commander, must outmaneuver a growing array of enemies as he prepares for an unequal showdown with Arvenon's invaders. Thomas, hunted unceasingly, must sacrifice all to safeguard the stone.

The fate of kingdoms soon hinges on them as they confront a ruthless invader hiding a darker purpose.

The odds are hopeless. And for three kingdoms, the stakes are higher than anyone knows.

The invasion is over, and the shattered Rogandan army has straggled home. The people of Arvenon and the surrounding kingdoms are at peace. Or so they believe.

Little do they know that a new stone of power has emerged, controlled by a cruel tyrant bent on destruction. But King Agon of Rogand lusts after much more than conquest. He will settle for nothing less than unending power.

No armies are massing at the border. The threat to the kingdom comes from within.

As chaos spreads, Will, Steffan, Essanda, and Arvenon's other key defenders are each confronted with crisis. If any one of them stumbles, the kingdom will fall.

To be kept up to date on new releases, sign up to my mailing list at *allanpacker.com*. New subscribers will receive an exclusive bonus novelette, *The Rending: A Prequel to The Cost of Knowing*, a complete story four chapters (13,000 words) in length. It provides additional context to one of the story threads from *The Cost of Knowing* without introducing spoilers for other books in *The Stone Cycle* series. The novelette is described below.

Endings may be beginnings in disguise

Anneka is comfortable and confident, a noblewoman of consequence living a life of privilege. Until the day her world is torn apart.

After losing everything she most cares about, she must abandon her home and her way of life in an attempt to secure the future of those who depend on her.

No one, least of all Anneka, could anticipate a deeper significance to her struggle. Yet her journey will one day influence the fate of kingdoms.

ACKNOWLEDGMENTS

Special thanks to my beta readers, Merilyn, Ray, Stephen, Deborah, James, Cherilyn White, and Melanie. They offered useful feedback and suggestions for improvements. Once again I greatly appreciated Deborah's thorough proofreading.

My grateful thanks go to Brian Plush for the awesome map.

Finally, thanks go to God, the source of creativity.

ABOUT THE AUTHOR

Allan Packer is an emerging author of epic fantasy. *The Seer* is his second novelette, following his novels *The Stone of Knowing* and *The Cost of Knowing*.

Allan grew up surrounded by books and became an avid reader during his childhood. In his university years fantasy displaced science fiction as his favorite genre, thanks primarily to J. R. R. Tolkien. He later shared this love with his four children by reading *The Lord of the Rings* to them aloud—a three-month marathon he completed twice during their formative years.

Born in Australia, Allan has lived and worked on three continents, and spent one quarter of his working years abroad. Having worked as an IT professional throughout his career, he was first published as a technical author.

Today he lives with his wife in Adelaide, South Australia, near their children and a small but growing band of grandchildren.

Allan is currently working on the next installment in his series *The Stone Cycle*.

facebook.com/allan.n.packer

amazon.com/author/allanpacker

bookbub.com/authors/allan-n-packer